"This is a *play*, Robin," said remaining patient. Everyor proper line, in turn, without making things up or finishing off the last person's—"

"Sandwich?"

"No."

"Pop?"

"No."

"Banana?"

"Robin!" Miss Everdue finally stamped a foot. She was used to Robin's habit of interrupting, but if she had been a kettle just then, steam might well have been blowing from her mouth.

YOUNG CORGI BOOKS

Young Corgi books are perfect when you are looking
for great books to read on your own. They are full of
exciting stories and entertaining pictures. There are
funny books, scary books, spine-tingling stories and
mysterious ones. Whatever your interests you'll find
something in Young Corgi to suit you, from
families to football, from animals to ghosts.
The books are written by some of the most famous
and popular of today's children's authors, and by
some of the best new talents, too.

Whether you read one chapter a night, or devour
the whole book in one sitting, you'll love
Young Corgi books. The more you read,
the more you'll want to read!

Other Young Corgi Books to get your teeth into:
THE RAILWAY ANGEL by Joyce Dunbar
TITUS RULES OK! by Dick King-Smith
SPUD by Alison Prince

THE PROMPTER

CHRIS D'LACEY

Illustrated by Ella Okstad

THE PROMPTER
A YOUNG CORGI BOOK 978 0 552 56419 9
Published by Young Corgi
An imprint of Random House Children's Books
A Random House Group Company

First published by Young Corgi in 2003
This edition published 2011

1 3 5 7 9 10 8 6 4 2

Text copyright © Chris d'Lacey, 2003
Illustrations copyright © Ella Okstad, 2003

The right of Chris d'Lacey to be identified as the author of this work has been
asserted in accordance with the Copyright, Designs and Patents Act 1988.

All rights reserved. No part of this publication may be reproduced, stored in a
retrieval system, or transmitted in any form or by any means, electronic,
mechanical, photocopying, recording or otherwise, without the prior permission of
the publishers.

The Random House Group Limited supports the Forest Stewardship Council (FSC),
the leading international forest certification organization. All our titles that are
printed on Greenpeace-approved FSC-certified paper carry the FSC logo. Our paper
procurement policy can be found at www.rbooks.co.uk/environment.

Mixed Sources
Product group from well-managed
forests and other controlled sources
www.fsc.org Cert no. TT-COC-2139
© 1996 Forest Stewardship Council

Set in 16/20pt Bembo Schoolbook by Falcon Oast Graphic Art Ltd.

Young Corgi Books are published by Random House Children's Books,
61-63 Uxbridge Road, London W5 5SA

www.kidsatrandomhouse.co.uk
www.rbooks.co.uk

Addresses for companies within The Random House Group Limited can be found
at: www.randomhouse.co.uk/offices.htm

THE RANDOM HOUSE GROUP Limited Reg. No. 954009

A CIP catalogue record for this book is available from the British Library.

Printed in the UK by CPI Cox & Wyman, Reading, RG1 8EX

For Audrey Willsher,
who prompted me to write it

Wonderful news!

The school play
is upon us again!

This year we are performing

Peter Pan

If you would like to take part,
please write your name on the list
and come along to the hall after
school on Wednesday.

Thank you,
Miss Everdue

Harmony Willow (and Rhiannon)

Eric Dibble

Sian Hooper

Aaron Cummings

Stephen Hitchcock

Robin Oakley — No Way

CHAPTER ONE

"Children," said Miss Everdue, clasping her delicate hands together, "thank you all for coming to the hall today. Welcome to the auditions for this year's play. Now, before we start, who remembers the story of Peter Pan?"

A girl with her hair in a ponytail cocked her hip and raised a hand.

"Yes, Harmony?"

Harmony Willow wiggled her nose. She did not explain the story of Peter Pan. She tilted her head towards a boy called Robin Oakley and said in a very petulant voice, "Miss, what's *he* doing here?"

"I've come to be in the play," said Robin. He pushed his way to the front of the group, lifted his arms and let them flop against his sides. He was a cheery, if slightly untidy lad. He looked for all the world as if he'd been posted and the envelope had got a little battered in the box. His hair grew in tufts at jerky little angles, as if it were made from stiff old paintbrushes. There were holes in his jumper and his collar was bent. His grey school trousers were stitched across the knees. But when he smiled, his mouth seemed to buckle at the corners and his freckles almost danced around his nose. It was fair to say he could be quite a challenge, but Miss Everdue felt he had lots of potential and always tried to encourage him. Harmony Willow did not.

"You *can't* be in the play. You'll ruin it," she snapped. "Miss, he'll be hopeless. He'll start doing—"

"I won't," said Robin, cutting Harmony off. He turned to Miss Everdue. "Can I be Peter the Pirate, miss?"

Harmony rolled her eyes.

Miss Everdue took a tissue from her sleeve and blew her nose with a faint little squeak. "Peter isn't actually a pirate, Robin. He's a boy who doesn't want to grow up."

"He'll be *perfect*, then," Harmony said unkindly. Her friend, Rhiannon, snickered into her fist. Harmony examined her fingernails and said, "Give him a line to say, go on. Bet you he messes it up."

Robin jumped up and down in delight.

"Well," said Miss Everdue, shuffling her script, "the role of Peter might be a little ambitious for you, Robin. But there *are* some pirate characters in the play. Why don't we try you out as one?

Can you picture a pirate ship in your mind?"

Robin jumped onto a long, low bench. "Like this one, miss?"

Several children laughed. Harmony sighed and groomed her hair (Rhiannon sighed too and held the mirror for her).

Miss Everdue glided across the floor, waving her arms in a theatrical fashion. "A-haar! Well improvised, Robin. Now, imagine that a battle is taking place. There is thick grey cannon smoke everywhere! You can taste its bitterness on your tongue. Cutlasses are clinking and clashing all around you. Suddenly, the dreaded Captain Hook appears. He turns to his motley crew and bellows—"

"We want fish fingers for dinner!"
(Robin bellowed.)

The children burst out laughing.

"See. He's doing it," Harmony said,
twizzling the end of her ponytail around
one finger. Rhiannon nodded. She
twizzled her hair too.

"No, no," said Miss Everdue, rustling
the script. "That's not the line, Robin.
Captain Hook speaks first and then *you*
have to say—"

"Puddles!" laughed Robin. It was his
favourite word.

"No," said Miss Everdue, remaining patient. "This is a *play*, Robin. Everyone has to speak the proper line, in turn, without making things up or finishing off the last person's—"

"Sandwich?"

"No."

"Pop?"

"No."

"Banana?"

"Robin!" Miss Everdue finally stamped a foot. She was used to Robin's habit of interrupting, but if she had been a kettle just then, steam might well have been blowing from her mouth. "Read *this*," she insisted, and pointed to the script.

Robin shook his head.

Miss Everdue frowned. "Why not? You're a very good reader."

Robin waved his hands in front of his face. "I can't see for the cannon smoke, miss."

Harmony slapped a hand to her brow. Rhiannon was barely half a second behind her.

Not to be defeated, Miss Everdue took a highlighter pen from her pocket and stroked it over part of the page. "Robin, this is a magic pen. It helps you to see through cannon smoke. Just read the pink words in a big, bold voice."

"Look out, it's the crocodile!" Robin yelled, pronouncing the words so big and so bold that Sian Hooper squealed and turned her knees inwards. Robin pointed fiercely towards the hall doors. Mrs Meredith, the headmistress, had just walked in!

"Did that child just call me a *crocodile*?" she snapped.

Miss Everdue let out an embarrassed laugh. "He was acting, Mrs Meredith. Robin is a pirate."

"I'm walking the plank!" the pirate shouted. And he strolled to the end of the long low bench, pinched his nose . . . and jumped.

Although the drop was only centimetres and the "water" was of course the floor of the hall, Robin entered the "ocean" with a mighty splash. He flopped onto his front, pretending to swim, then shouted, "Oh no, the jellyfish has got me!"

He wrestled for a moment with an imaginary jellyfish, made gurgling noises, then lay outstretched on his back, quite still.

One or two children clapped his performance. Mrs Meredith stopped them with an icy glare. She drew Miss Everdue aside. "I don't think Robin Oakley is suitable material for something as important as the school play, do you?"

Miss Everdue raised her chin. She was a tall young woman, like a fresh blade of grass. She swayed sometimes when she spoke. "Robin is auditioning, like the other children. It would not be fair to keep him out. I know he's a little . . . excitable at times, but that doesn't mean he cannot act."

"Excitable?" Mrs Meredith repeated. One of her eyebrows began to jiggle as though an unseen hand was working it with strings. "That boy won't speak one line of your play without doing . . . you know what."

"I shall prove you wrong," Miss Everdue said boldly. "Robin, can you stand up now, please?"

"Can't, miss. The jellyfish have stung me. Urrk!"

Mrs Meredith glowered. "And since when were there jellyfish in Peter Pan?"

Miss Everdue looked at Robin and sighed. "Give me time, Mrs Meredith. Just give me time."

CHAPTER TWO

The auditions went as well as could be
expected. However, by the end of the
session Miss Everdue was still undecided
about which children should play which
roles, apart from Harmony Willow, that
is. Harmony, who could dance like her
favourite pop star and sing so loudly
that it deafened Sian Hooper, had given
a stirring performance as Tinker Bell
the fairy (with Rhiannon as the fairy's
helper). When Miss Everdue had
explained that the part of Tinker Bell

was terribly dramatic and that at one point in the play Tink might die if children didn't clap their hands to show they truly believed in fairies, Harmony had swooned to the ground and lay there as limp as a piece of fluff. Her performance was so convincing that Robin had needed to toe-poke her

(gently) just to make sure she wasn't *really* dead. Harmony's snarl of "Watch it, Oakley!" had quickly established the presence of life, but she had still insisted on some thunderous clapping before she would rise to her feet once more.

And so it was arranged that the group would meet again the following afternoon, when Miss Everdue would announce who would play the other parts. The children drifted happily away, all except Robin, whom Miss Everdue beckoned into the school office. She placed her script in the large grey photocopier and a neat new copy squirted out into the tray. "There," she said, handing it over. "I want you to—"

"Colour it in? Do drawings on it, miss?"

"No," said Miss Everdue, lifting a finger, a sign that Robin was not to interrupt. "Take it home and *read it*, Robin."

"Under the blanket with a torch, Miss Everdue? Just in case the crocodile comes?"

Miss Everdue gave him a look. Robin bit his lip and fell silent a moment. Miss Everdue dropped the manuscript into an envelope. "Ask your mother or father to read the play with you. Take your time and concentrate. One thing we must learn in life is that we should only speak when we are spoken to, especially when performing a play. You showed great enthusiasm in the auditions. I don't think I can cast you as Peter Pan or Hook, but with practice you might do well as Smee."

"As *you*?" said Robin, with a jolt of surprise. "Are *you* in the play, miss?"

Miss Everdue counted patiently to three. "No, Robin, not *me*. The pirate, *Smee*."

The freckles danced on Robin's face. "Do a pirate voice, miss!"

Miss Everdue did not do a pirate voice. She picked up a pen and hurriedly wrote, "*Dear Mrs Oakley, Robin is trying for the part of Smee*" on the back of the envelope. She all but stapled it to Robin's jumper. "You'll understand when you read it," she said. And she showed him into the corridor.

Robin stumbled forward, then broke into a run. "Look out, it's the crocodile!" he shouted as he went, swishing an imaginary cutlass through the air. Sian Hooper, who was feeding the school fish some flakes, almost jumped into the aquarium in shock.

Mrs Meredith poked her head into the corridor to see what all the noise was about. She stared beadily in Miss Everdue's direction.

"Just rehearsing, Mrs M," Miss Everdue twittered.

Mrs Meredith scowled and slid back into her office.

Not unlike a crocodile, in fact.

CHAPTER THREE

When Robin and his mum arrived
home from school, Robin's dad was
busy in his garden workshop. Mr
Oakley made guitars and violins for a
living. His workshop, which was really
little more than a shed, was full of
interesting pieces of wood. It smelled of
varnish and resin and glue, and the
floor was a sea of curly wood shavings.

Mr Oakley was working at his
sanding wheel when Robin came
bursting in. The buzz of the machine
drowned all of Robin's chatter. He was

hoarse and breathless by the time Mr Oakley was aware of his presence and had switched off the sander to listen.

Mr Oakley wiped his hands against his brown leather apron and pushed his safety goggles onto his brow. "What did you say, son?"

"Dad," Robin panted, blowing wood motes into clouds. "I'm in the school play. I'm going to be—"

"A shepherd?" Mr Oakley guessed.

Robin coughed and shook his head.

"An alien?"

"No, Dad."

"An astronaut?"

"No."

"A pantomime horse? Which end are you?"

Robin snorted like a horse at that.

Mr Oakley guessed on: "An acrobat? A chimney sweep? A big furry rabbit?"

"No," laughed Robin, giving his dad a slap. "A pirate, Dad."

"A pirate?!" Mr Oakley cried, standing very tall with his feet wide apart and his fists on his hips. "Shiver me timbers! Rattle me bones! Where be your cutlass, Master Oakley?"

Robin picked up the neck of a guitar. "Here, Dad!"

Mr Oakley closed one eye. "That be no cutlass," he said in a growl. "You couldn't chop a choc chip cookie with that. Cross my palm with salty spit and I be making 'ee a blade that be the envy of buccaneers the seven seas over."

Robin spat into the centre of his hand and slapped it hard against his father's palm.

"Aar," went Mr Oakley with a piratey grimace. He twisted Robin round and spoke in a low voice into his ear. "You be telling your mother I be taking my tea in this shack tonight, while I be working on your trusty blade. Be saying aye aye."

"Aye aye," said Robin.

"Away with 'ee, then!" Mr Oakley bellowed. He tousled Robin's hair and pointed to the door.

"Look out, it's the crocodile!" Robin shouted happily and pelted up the garden path.

Mr Oakley raised a dusty eyebrow. "Crocodile?" he muttered. "You be

needing a right good blade for that."
And he chose a piece of balsa wood
from a pile in the corner and started to
draw out the shape of a cutlass.

Mrs Oakley was no less inspired by
Robin's venture. "You must have a
proper costume," she declared. And so,
after tea, she made Robin put on an old
pair of jeans, which she cut off at the
knees with a special pair of scissors that
made an interesting zigzag trim. Then
she found one of Mr Oakley's old shirts.
It billowed like a sail against Robin's
chest. There were cufflinks in the sleeves
and lace about the collar. Mrs Oakley
said that was the pirate fashion. All
Robin needed now, she added, was an
earring and a headscarf . . . and possibly
a parrot. Robin's eyes lit up like stars.
Mrs Oakley said she would work on the
parrot. The headscarf she could make
from a tea-towel by morning.

But that night they sat and read the script. Not once, not twice, but *three* times in all. (The last time while Robin was tucked up in bed.) While Mr Oakley worked on the cutlass, shaping and sanding till moths fluttered round his hanging lamp, Robin and his mother studied the play.

They learned that Peter Pan was the captain of a group of boys, who had all fallen out of their prams as babies and gone unclaimed by their parents! They were called the Lost Boys, and they had all been sent to Neverland, an island

that could be whatever you imagined.
There were pirates on the island – lots
of them – the dreadful Captain Hook
for one, whose right hand had been
eaten by a crocodile!

Robin liked the crocodile. It wanted
to gobble up the rest of Captain Hook.
But it had never
been able to
catch him
again. This
was because
it had
swallowed a
clock and the
ticking always
warned Hook
when the croc
was near.

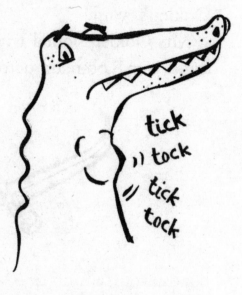

"Bit like your father when he burps,"
said Mrs Oakley.

Robin would normally have laughed
at that. But the stars were out and he

was tired now. Mrs Oakley, knowing it, stood up gently and let Robin's head fall against the pillow. He was snoring softly when his dad tiptoed in and laid a painted wooden cutlass at the foot of the bed. Mr Oakley saluted his son. "Night, night, shipmate," he whispered, and slipped an arm around Mrs Oakley's waist.

Mrs Oakley sighed with joy. "Just think, our Robin, an actor," she said.

CHAPTER FOUR

Robin's cutlass was the talk of the
school the next day. Stephen Hitchcock
wanted to swap it for some conkers.
Several children asked: if they became
pirates, would Robin's dad make a
cutlass for them? That thought was also
on Miss Everdue's mind. She said the
cutlass was splendid. She asked Robin to
ask his dad if he might help out with
the scenery, generally. Robin grinned so
much his freckles almost popped. He
wasn't used to being so popular – that
role belonged to Harmony Willow.

"Huh," she told Rhiannon. "I'll show that Robin Oakley." And the next day she turned up with wings on her back. Not real wings, of course. They were made of golden paper and fluttered when she moved. She also wore a bright pink ballet skirt with a short lace train for Rhiannon to hold. But the best part of her outfit was undoubtedly her hat. It looked like a bluebell flower. Inside it

 was a small yellow light. It twinkled when she danced, making patterns on the ceiling. The children clapped and gasped in astonishment. It was just as though Tinker Bell was truly among them.

But wonderful outfits and painted pirate swords would not by themselves make a play, said Miss Everdue. There was much hard work to be done. And so, as the days went by, she coached the children gently with their lines. Robin, who now understood that Smee was a pirate, did not have much to do in the early stages. To keep him happy, Miss Everdue allowed him to practise sword fights with other pirates. Only once did these "rehearsals" end in bad temper, when Stephen Hitchcock charged at Robin, who repelled his lunge with a dinner tray and bent Stephen's plastic sword in the process.

But in time there came a scene for Robin to be part of. In Act Two, Peter Pan had led a girl called Wendy to Neverland. When they arrived, they had to hide from the pirates. The pirates, who consisted of Robin, Stephen and a boy called Eric Dibble (who was playing Captain Hook), had to stamp across the hall looking mean and frightening. Robin was rather good at this. So good, in fact, that Miss Everdue had to tell him not to stamp so hard lest he break the stage on opening night.

Nor was he allowed to grind his teeth, because the sound made Sian feel "wobbly sick". But it was not the stamping or the grinding which caused the great falling out with Harmony. While Peter and Wendy were hiding from the pirates, Tinker Bell was flitting mischievously about. Harmony's interpretation of "flitting" was to twirl on her toes like a ballet dancer and sweep back and forth in full view of everyone.

Peter called, "Tink, fly higher. They'll catch you, for sure."

Captain Hook said, "Boys, did you see that light?"

Tinker Bell said, "I am tiny. So tiny they cannot see me."

"I can!" said Robin and jabbed his cutlass through her wing.

Pandemonium followed. Harmony, incensed by this unprovoked attack, swung a hard kick at Robin's knees. Immediately, there came a ripping sound. A somewhat surprised Rhiannon found herself holding Harmony's skirt. Harmony, embarrassed by the sudden exposure, covered her knickers and ran for the doors.

"Look out, it's the crocodile!" Robin shouted as Mrs Meredith, with perfect timing, walked in.

Harmony ploughed straight into her. The flower hat crumpled and the bulb exploded. It was a miserable end to the fairy's day.

Mrs Meredith was not amused. "Who caused this dreadful riot?" she snapped. Her gaze settled on Robin Oakley.

"A-haar," he said a bit weakly.

Mrs Meredith came up and whipped off his headscarf. "I might have known! What is the first rule of our school, Robin?"

"We must always be good to others, Mrs Meredith."

"Then why is Harmony's costume torn?"

Robin gave a nervous shrug.

"Give me that cutlass."

Robin handed it over.

Mrs Meredith took his parrot, too. "I will not permit children to pick on other pupils. Your acting days are over, my lad." She pointed to the doors. The gentle tick of her golden wristwatch echoed in the silent hollows of the hall.

Miss Everdue whispered, "You'd better go, Robin."

Robin lowered his head and walked.

"Aw," went someone, but it made no difference.

Robin was out of the play.

CHAPTER FIVE

Miss Everdue followed Robin outside.
She sat him down beneath a sycamore
tree and tried very hard to explain the
problem. A play was like the passage of
time, she said. Things had to progress in
a straightforward manner, one speech
after the other: tick, tock. If the
sequence of tocks and ticks was
disrupted, the story would not make
sense to the audience. Everyone would
be confused. It wasn't that Robin
couldn't *act*. Far from it. He was a jolly

good pirate. A seadog through and
through. But if he did the kind of thing
he had just done to Harmony when the
school, or even the parents, were
watching . . . well, there would be
uproar. Tomatoes might be thrown.
People might boo. And that would be an
end to school plays for ever.

Miss Everdue patted his arm. "I still
want to find a role for you, Robin, but
it won't be on the stage, I'm afraid. I
can't go against the headmistress.
Perhaps you might be involved in other
ways, like helping your father to build
the props?"

Robin dug his hands into the
comforting fluff of his trouser pockets.
His dad had agreed to make some
boards which could be slid across the
stage to create the scenery. It *was* an
exciting job, but nowhere near as good
as the stamping and grinding he'd done
as a pirate. With a sigh he stood up.

There was a leaf in his hair and a feather in his jumper. But the downward twist to his mouth said it all: there was no joy in his sad little heart.

The next few days were hard. Miss Everdue wrote a letter to Robin's parents expressing her disappointment at Mrs Meredith's decision and saying she would personally do all she could to keep young Robin involved with the project. Mr and Mrs Oakley took it in their stride. It was not the first time that Robin's eccentricities had seen him cast aside from school events.

As for Robin, he could still be seen now and then, nose pressed up against the cold hall windows, watching the rehearsals from the yard outside. It quite unnerved Miss Harmony Willow, who strode across the hall one dark afternoon and in a great fury shouted, "Oh, go away, you sneaky *ghost!*"

It was a horrible thing to say and Miss Everdue knew it. "Oh, Harmony!" she stormed. "Don't be such a dreadful prima donna!"

"Prima who?" said Stephen Hitchcock to Eric Dibble.

Eric Dibble waved his hook and nearly got it caught in his curly captain's wig. "He played for Italy in the World Cup, I think."

Prima donna or not, Harmony Willow was the star of the show. She knew it. The whole school knew it. To be fair, they had very little choice in the matter. Harmony liked to practise her lines, loudly and dramatically, wherever she went. And woe betide anyone who dared to interrupt . . .

Of course, it had to happen. One break time she was practising with Peter and Wendy at the back of Mrs Simpson's art and crafts room. Robin was at a desk, drawing pictures of pirates, when the impromptu rehearsal began.

"Right," said Harmony. "We'll do the bit where I go into Wendy's bedroom looking for Peter's shadow and he shuts me in a drawer by mistake." And away she went, flitting round the desks, Rhiannon "helping" as always. "Oh, look at this *awful* bedroom," she simpered. "It's quite full of . . ." Strangely, there was a silent pause.

Harmony frowned and put a hand to her head. "It's quite full of . . ."

"Dog hair," said a voice. Robin's voice. He hadn't turned round or looked up from his drawing. Neither was he aware that Miss Everdue was sitting out of sight round the corner. She lifted her head to hear what was happening.

"Shut up!" said Harmony. "Who asked you?" She threw an eraser at Robin's back. It bounced off his shoulder and landed in Sian Hooper's sandwich box.

"He's right, though," said Wendy, in a timid little voice. "The room *is* supposed to be full of dog hairs."

"I *know-ww*," said Harmony. "I would have said, *eventually*. I'm just not feeling very well today." She gave her ponytail a petulant flick. Rhiannon, whose hair was rather too short for flicking, merely stamped her foot.

Wendy, deciding that the show must go on, clasped her hands together and said, "Oh, who is this at my windowsill?"

"I am Peter Pan," said Peter.

"Where do you come from?" Wendy asked him.

"Neverland."

"Oh, how do you get *there*?"

Peter opened his mouth to speak, but he too seemed to have forgotten his words.

"Well, tell her," hissed Harmony, gritting her teeth.

"It's . . ." Peter started.

"Oh," went Harmony impatiently. "It's the third star on the left and then straight on till morning."

"'Tisn't," said Robin, shaking his head. "It's the *second* star on the *right*. That's how you fly to Neverland."

"Quite right," Miss Everdue whispered to herself. "Well done, Robin."

Harmony Willow took the opposite view. She marched up and knocked Robin's pencil from his hand. "Go away. I can't say my lines properly with *you* sitting there."

"You don't have to," Robin defended stoutly. "You don't say anything for ages yet. You just go '*Nee nee nee*' in a squeaky fairy voice and call Wendy a great big ugly girl."

"I don't like that bit," said Wendy.

"Well," said Harmony, making a face, "you're not exactly pretty, are you?"

At that, Wendy turned away and left the room in tears.

"Oh," went Harmony, in a proper huff. "Now I can't practise *anything*."

"You don't have to, you're locked in a drawer," said Robin.

Harmony drew in her shoulders. She pushed up her sleeves in a threatening manner and looked as if she might give Robin a punch. Fortunately, Miss Everdue appeared at that moment. "Harmony, stop scowling and behave yourself. You're acting like a very spoiled little girl. If I hear any more of it, you'll be out of the play."

"Oh, mi–iss?"

"That's enough. I want to talk to Robin."

Pouting, Harmony held out her hand. Rhiannon promptly put a tissue in it.

Miss Everdue turned to Robin. "How did you remember those lines so well?"

Robin crunkled his lip and lifted a shoulder.

Miss Everdue tapped her chin in thought. "Tell me, which line comes after this? 'I am James Hook, Captain of the *Jolly Roger* pirate ship.'"

"And I am a codfish!" Robin announced. "Peter says it, miss, to tease the captain and make him mad."

Harmony tutted under her breath. But tut all she liked, even she could not deny that as strange as Robin's answer seemed, it was, in fact, correct.

A slow smile spread across Miss Everdue's face. "Well, odds, bobs, hammer

and tongs, as Captain Hook himself might have said. Congratulations, Robin, you're back in the play."

"What?!" screeched Harmony. "Which part is he playing?"

"All of them and none," Miss Everdue said as though she were giving out a riddle. "Robin is going to be our prompter."

CHAPTER SIX

Mrs Meredith turned quite pale at the news. "Prompter?" she hissed, baring her teeth. "That's all that child *ever* does is prompt."

"Quite so," said Miss Everdue, with a slight air of triumph. "But no one, not even you, Headmistress, can deny that Robin will have *good cause* to interrupt, for once. Every play needs a prompter, and Robin is ours."

Mrs Meredith wrinkled her nose. Her wispy brown eyebrows were drawn into a frown and her lips were as straight as railway tracks. "I don't like it. He's sure to mess things up."

Miss Everdue took a defiant stand. She removed her glasses and polished them hard. "Robin has a photographic memory," she said. "Any child of his age who can remember a whole play word for word should be congratulated and encouraged, not treated with suspicion. I am confident he will do a very fine job." And with the tiniest of hmphs! she swept away, fingers tightly crossed.

For, in truth, even she could not be sure that Robin would not make a hash of things. But time was short, today was Wednesday, tomorrow was the dress rehearsal and Friday was the day of the play. The show must go on. Worrying could not be part of the script.

As it happened, Miss Everdue's concerns were quickly forgotten. On the day of the dress rehearsal, Robin stood in the wings of the stage, dutifully

following the
play from the
script. He didn't
actually *need* a
script. He really
did know the
play off by heart.
But Miss Everdue
felt it would
help him to
concentrate if he
followed the lines
word for word on
the page. And
concentrate he
did. Only once
did he speak up a
little too quickly
when Harmony paused for dramatic
effect and, in her opinion, completely
ruined the "emotion of the moment".

Otherwise, the rehearsal went very
well. The costumes were splendid.

The performances spectacular. The only actor who seemed a little out of sorts was Aaron Cummings. Aaron was playing the role of the crocodile. With the help of several children in her class, Miss Everdue had constructed a magnificent crocodile head from papier-mâché, which Aaron was wearing for the first time that day. It was a little

stuffy inside the head and Aaron had been having slight problems at first seeing through the eye holes (in the crocodile's jaw). Everyone imagined that the combination of restricted vision and the sweltering atmosphere inside the head had been the reason for Aaron's impressive waddling. But as the rehearsal was coming to a close, there was a clatter from the back of the stage. Aaron had fallen down the stage steps.

There were only five steps so the fall wasn't bad. But as Aaron stood up and removed the croc's head he reeled and fell into Miss Everdue's arms.

"Aaron, whatever happened?" she cried, sitting him down and fanning his face.

"Feel dizzy," he said, and his head flopped forward.

"Robin," called Miss Everdue, "run to the staff room and fetch—"

"Water, miss?"

"Yes, and—"

"A tissue?"

"Yes, and—"

"Some plasters, miss?"

"No, not plasters."

"Oh, shut up, freckle-face!" Harmony cut in, trying to shove Robin aside.

Robin pushed her back. "Get lost, spotty!"

"I do not have spots!" stormed Harmony.

"Yes, you do," said Steven Hitchcock,
matter-of-factly, waving his cutlass in
Harmony's face.

Rhiannon let out a horrified gasp.

"Children, what on earth is going
on?" asked Miss Everdue, cradling
Aaron's head against her shoulder.

Sian Hooper bent down and
whispered in her ear.

A look of shock passed over Miss
Everdue's face. "Harmony, let me look
at you." Harmony knelt down. Miss

Everdue examined her forehead and cheeks. She tilted Aaron's face up to the light.

"Aaron's got spots as well," said Robin.

"Not spots," said Miss Everdue, sighing deeply. "I'm afraid that's chickenpox."

CHAPTER SEVEN

Three children had the infection: Aaron Cummings, the crocodile; Harmony Willow, Tinker Bell; and Eric Dibble, who played Captain Hook.

For Harmony, it was all too much. "My career is over," she squawked. She switched off her light and let her paper wings droop. A fairy tear rolled down her pale pink cheek. "How long does it take to get rid of them, miss?" (She meant the spots, of course.)

"Seven to ten days," Miss Everdue said.

"But that's after the end of term," said Harmony. "Are we going to do the play next term instead?"

Miss Everdue frowned in thought. "Children, put up your hand if you've already had the chickenpox."

Nearly everyone raised their hand.

"Splendid," said Miss Everdue. "We must check you all, of course, but if those of you with hands raised are correct, you are safe; it's unlikely that you would catch chickenpox again. Therefore, the show might yet go on!"

"Without *me*?" screeched Harmony. "But who's going to be Tinker Bell?"

Miss Everdue looked over Harmony's shoulder. "Rhiannon."

"Uh?" went Harmony, her mouth like a cave. "Rhiannon's my *helper*. She can't do it! She doesn't talk anyway. She only ever mumbles."

To everyone's surprise (Harmony's especially), Rhiannon hurried forward and bumped her best friend out of the way. "I *can* do it, miss. Honestly, I can."

"You have to sing," said Stephen.

"And flit," said Robin.

"I know," said a very excited Rhiannon. And away she went, flitting and singing as if she were born to the part of Tink.

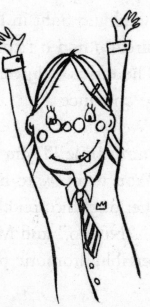

Harmony Willow bawled like a baby. "It's not fair," she stamped.

"Come along," said Miss Everdue, guiding Harmony and Eric and a slightly befuddled Aaron Cummings to the door. "Let's get you to the staff room and ring your parents."

Stephen Hitchcock skidded up to her side. "But, miss, who's going to play Captain Hook – and the crocodile?"

Miss Everdue raised her chin. "I'll think about it," she said a little secretively. But it was clear from the twinkling light in her eye that she already had a firm plan worked out. There was only one person she needed to convince . . .

"Crocodile?!" Mrs Meredith boomed. "You want *me* to be a crocodile? I'll be the laughing stock of the school!"

"No, no," said Miss Everdue. "It's a terribly dramatic part, Mrs Meredith.

And it would go down awfully well with the governors, all of whom will be in the audience, to know that the head was involving herself at a moment of crisis."

Mrs Meredith rubbed her chin. "Hmm, very well. What do I have to say?"

"'Tick tock, tick tock, here I come around the clock. I bit the hand of Captain Hook. Now I want the rest, yuk, yuk!'"

"Yuk, yuk?" Mrs Meredith repeated.

"It sort of rhymes," said Miss Everdue.

"I know that," snapped the head.

"Write it down. I'll need to practise."

Miss Everdue scribbled the rhyme onto a piece of paper.

As she did so, Mrs Meredith raised another question. "Just a minute, I haven't rehearsed. How will I know when to make an appearance?"

"You'll be prompted."

"By the Oakley boy?"

"Erm, yes." Miss Everdue reddened slightly. "Robin is still the prompt."

"Hmm," Mrs Meredith rumbled. "Well, he'd better not mess me around. Who's playing Hook?"

Miss Everdue slipped towards the door. "The . . . erm . . . understudy," she said. "He's very good . . . the understudy. I must go and speak to him . . . now! Goodbye!"

CHAPTER EIGHT

"Robin, this is your moment," said Miss Everdue. She was kneeling in front of him, clasping his hands. They were in the back room behind the hall where the children were changing into their costumes. In ten minutes' time, the play would begin. "All you have to do," Miss Everdue told him, "is speak the words like you did in the classroom, in the right order, the way they are here." She tapped the side of Robin's head, making him smile.

"But what about Mrs Meredith?" he asked. "Won't she be mad when she sees me, miss?"

Miss Everdue reached into her bag and drew out the wig for Captain Hook. It was black and curly, with flowing ringlets. She pulled it onto Robin's head. "This is a school emergency, Robin. Mrs Meredith will be pleased you're helping out. Anyway, she won't recognize you – not in your wig, with your make-up on." She opened some face paints and drew some bright red circles on Robin's cheeks. Then she taped a wavy moustache to his lip. "You look wonderful," she said. "Your parents will be so proud. They're in the audience, three rows back. Oh, that reminds me, speaking of your parents, I retrieved this from Mrs Meredith's room." She brought out the painted wooden cutlass that Mr Oakley had made some weeks before.

Robin took it and chanted, "A-haar!" (In the background, his crew all echoed the cry.)

"A-haar, indeed," Miss Everdue said. "Ooh, look out, here comes the crocodile."

Mrs Meredith had just entered the back of the room, the crocodile's head tucked under her arm. She was wearing a pair of bright-green tights which did little to contain her bulging bottom. Stephen Hitchcock said that in his opinion the tights were scarier than the crocodile's teeth, but no one dared snicker at the dreaded headmistress.

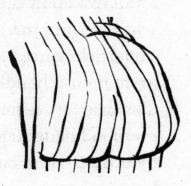

As the lights went down and the show began, Robin took his place in the wings. He was still the prompter, on stage or off. But that was his secondary task tonight. His leading role was the dreaded Captain Hook, and he played it with wonderful dash and verve. In the scene where he had to fight Peter Pan, several people gasped as his cutlass flashed and Peter's bright-green hat fell off! The audience were so impressed with his snarls that they joined in with good-natured hisses and boos. This only made Robin stamp his foot and shake his "iron claw" at them. The crowd loved this and clapped him loudly. And whenever the crocodile appeared on stage, ticking and tocking and wanting more than a hand, yuk, yuk, they would all shout: "It's behind you, run!" For everybody knew that the creature was after him, but nobody wanted to see him eaten up!

But the moment came at the end of
the play when the crocodile's famous
clock ran down. This meant it didn't tick
any more. This meant it could sneak up
on Captain Hook! Up it came from the
side of the stage. Robin (the captain)
was busy fighting Peter. And what's
more, Peter was winning. He had
knocked the captain's cutlass from his
hand. It was time for Captain Hook to

jump into the ocean and try to swim
away. But the crocodile was there! Yuk!
Yuk! As Robin turned round and
jumped off the plank that he and Peter
had been fighting on, he delivered his
last line perfectly, "Agh! It's the
crocodile for me!"

At this point, Mrs Meredith was supposed to make a great show of gobbling Robin up. But to everyone's surprise, she pointed a finger and snapped, "It's you!"

Robin's jump from the plank had been so jarring that his wavy moustache had tilted on his lip. Mrs Meredith had recognized him!

"Come here, you," she snarled.

"No, you'll never get me!" Robin cried. And picking up his cutlass, he jabbed Mrs Meredith once in the bottom, then ran for his life.

It was a scene to end all scenes. Robin hurried down the aisle between the rows of parents with the angry crocodile hard on his heels. The crowd clapped and urged him on. Some turned their programmes into paper planes and threw them as Mrs Meredith went past. A great cheer went up when she stumbled against the leg of a chair and went sliding along the polished hall floor like a giant green penguin, ending up crashing through the doors of the kitchen. Mrs Meredith was led away dizzied and humbled. She did not take her bow at the final curtain, but Robin Oakley did. When he took off his hat

and swept it low to the floor, the roar of
applause made the light fittings shudder.

"A-haar!" he cried.

"A-haar!" replied the crowd.

Quite the perfect prompt.

THE END